The Calico Jungle

Islandport Press, P.O. Box 10, Yarmouth, Maine 04096
www.islandportpress.com   books@islandportpress.com

The Calico Jungle was first published in 1965 by Alfred A. Knopf, Inc. This edition is
published by Islandport Press in cooperation with Dahlov Ipcar.

ISBN 978-1-934-031-31-5
Library of Congress Control Number 2010930028
Printed in Canada

For Barbara Emily,
who plays with calico animals and sleeps on a tiger-skin rug

The Calico

ISLANDPORT PRESS

YARMOUTH, MAINE

Jungle

written and illustrated by Dahlov Ipcar

Once there was a little boy whose mother made him a wonderful calico quilt for his bed. It was a beautiful quilt, all covered with jungle trees and flowers and animals.

Every night, after his mother tucked him
into bed and kissed him good night,
the little boy lay there in his bed, in the dim
evening light, and looked at all the animals
among the strange and wonderful trees.

Under the trees, calico flowers grew and calico
butterflies flew. And there were peacocks
and rabbits there.

Some of the animals were not easy to see. The little boy had to look hard to see the black-and-white zebras hiding among the tree trunks.

And he had to look carefully to see
the coily, spotted snake winding
its way through a tree full of
flowers and fruits.

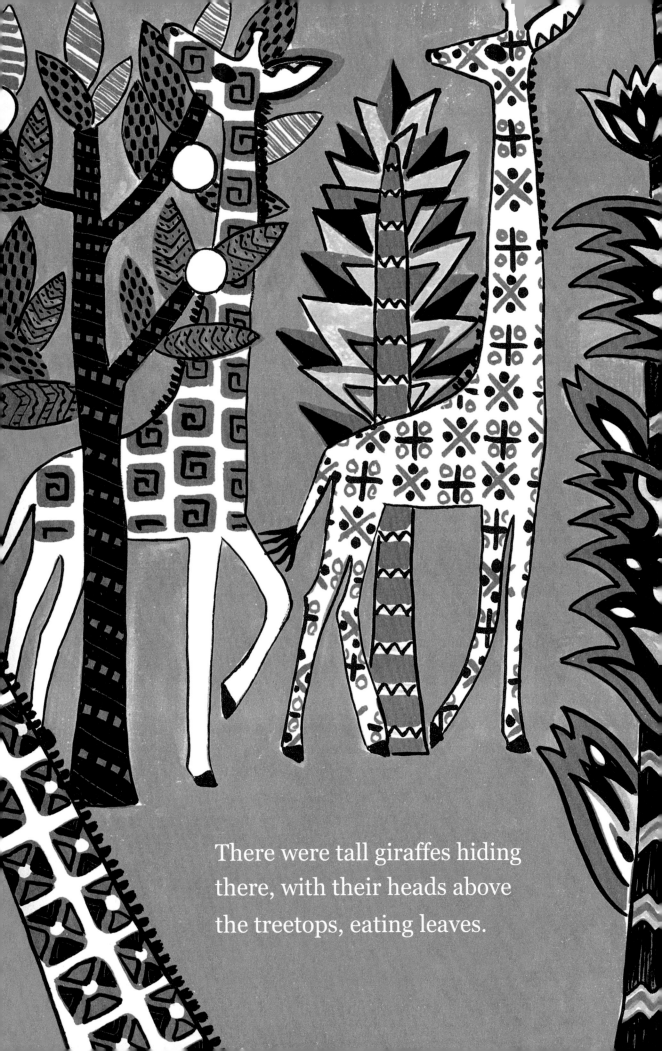

There were tall giraffes hiding there, with their heads above the treetops, eating leaves.

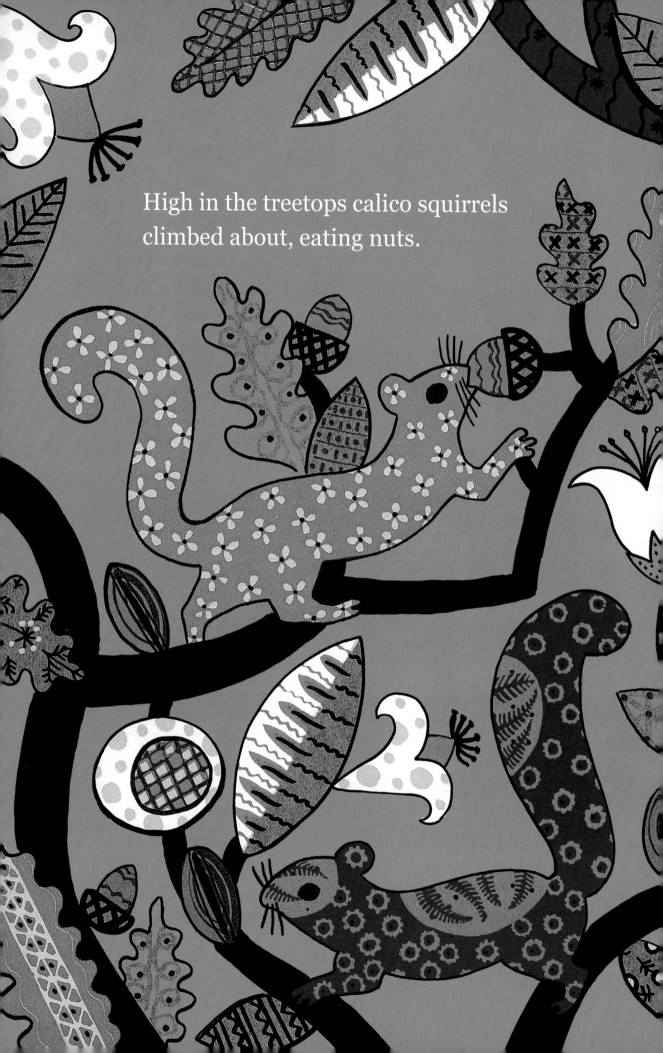

High in the treetops calico squirrels
climbed about, eating nuts.

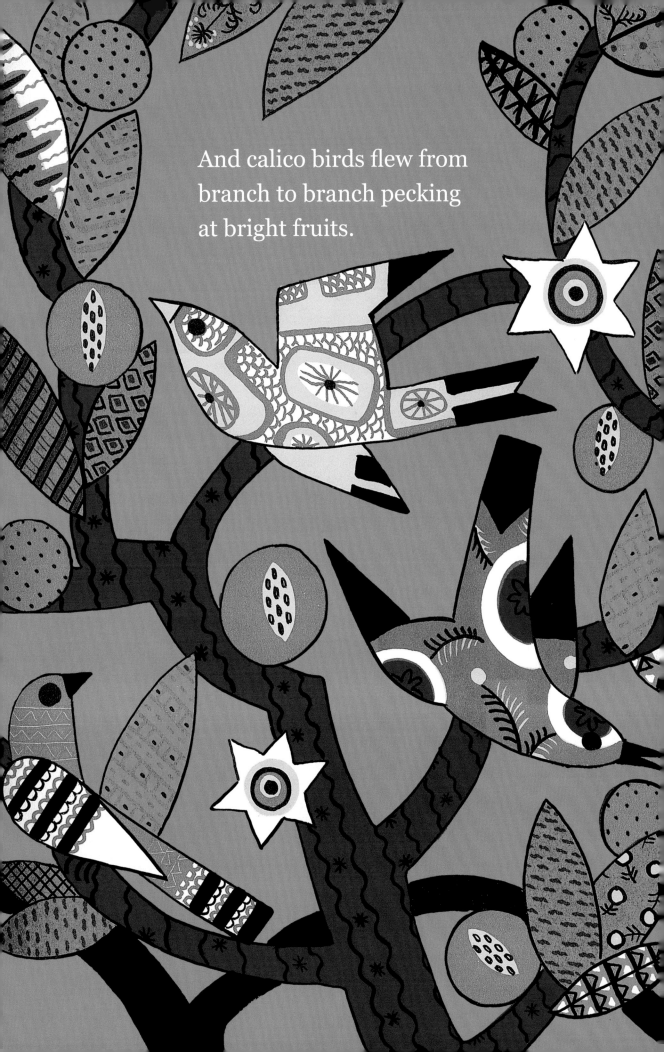

And calico birds flew from
branch to branch pecking
at bright fruits.

Some of the animals were easy to see,
such as a white unicorn and a big black
rhinoceros—each with one long horn.

Grazing among the trees were wild antelopes
with long horns.

Some of them were running away
to hide in the depths of the jungle.

And, in the very middle of the jungle, was a lovely, deep green pool.

There, big black elephants gave each other shower baths.

Fish swam in the pool,
calico fish with strange shapes
and bright colors, shining like
jewels in the rippling green water.

Fat black hippos splashed in the pool,
and big green crocodiles swam there.

Long-legged birds waded in the water, catching fish.

And all the animals came to the pool to drink.

And, deeper in the jungle, beyond the pool,
where it was quiet and dark and peaceful,
the little boy found a sleeping lion and a
sleeping tiger, and a small jungle cat
asleep under a bush.

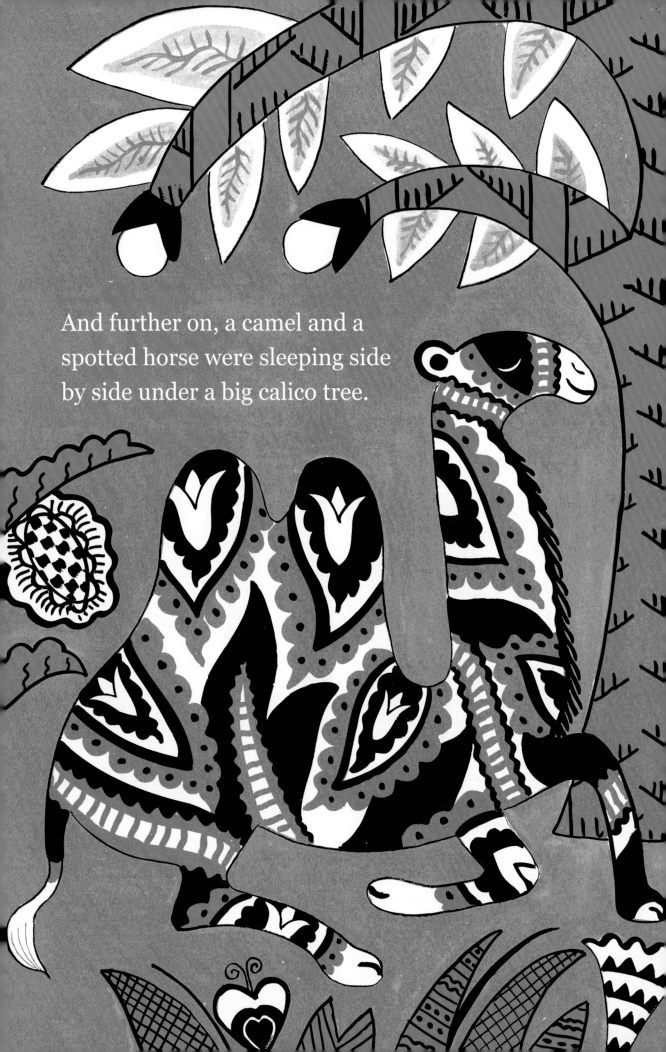

And further on, a camel and a spotted horse were sleeping side by side under a big calico tree.

And a small spotted dog was
curled up tight in a sleepy ball.

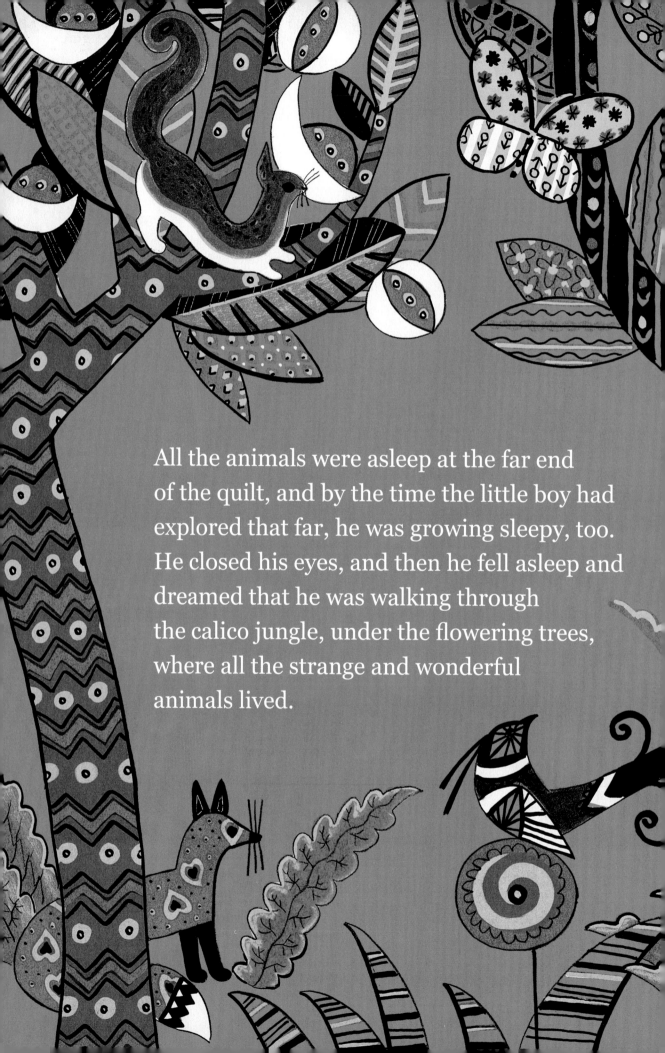

All the animals were asleep at the far end
of the quilt, and by the time the little boy had
explored that far, he was growing sleepy, too.
He closed his eyes, and then he fell asleep and
dreamed that he was walking through
the calico jungle, under the flowering trees,
where all the strange and wonderful
animals lived.

Dahlov Ipcar was born in Vermont in 1917. Raised in Greenwich Village, she summered in Maine after her parents (the famed sculptor William Zorach and artist Marguerite Zorach) bought a farm in Georgetown Island in 1923. Thirteen years later, eighteen-year-old Dahlov, an aspiring artist, married Adolph Ipcar. The young couple left New York City in 1937 to live on the Maine farm where they first met.

By the early 1940s, though she was starting to establish herself as a painter, Dahlov had nearly given up thoughts of writing and illustrating books when she was contacted by a New York publisher to illustrate *The Little Fisherman,* written by Margaret Wise Brown. The struggling young artist jumped at the chance. This charming title, published in 1945, helped launch a four-decade run that saw her write and illustrate more than thirty children's books. In 2001, the Maine Library Association honored Dahlov with the Katahdin Award, a lifetime achievement award recognizing an outstanding body of work of children's literature in Maine.

In the milestone book, *The Calico Jungle,* first published in 1965, Dahlov was feeling the urge to express herself in a new way. The book's illustrations marked a dramatic change in style as she began to explore "the endless possibilities of patterns. It had a terrific influence on my fine art," she says. "It inspired me to change

OTHER ISLANDPORT PRESS TITLES
BY DAHLOV IPCAR

The Little Fisherman
(written by Margaret Wise Brown)

The Cat at Night

My Wonderful Christmas Tree

Hardscrabble Harvest

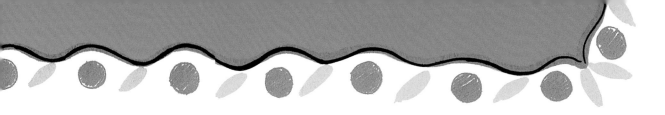

my whole style." *The Calico Jungle* is a shining example of her exploration into the juxtaposition of shapes, colors, patterns, and light, the hallmark of her later work.

Today, Dahlov's intricate, distinctive, and fanciful artwork is known worldwide, with pieces of her work in the collections of numerous renowned museums, including The Metropolitan Museum of Art and the Whitney Museum of American Art.

Though Dahlov has not illustrated a children's book since the 1980s, she remains a prolific artist. She lives and paints in the farmhouse that she shared with Adolph for nearly seventy years. She once said she didn't want celebrity or fame; she just "wanted to be recognized." In retrospect, a fairly modest statement for a Maine—and American—treasure.